The Portal Adventure
- Planet L23

The Portal Adventure-Planet L23

발 행 | 2023년 3월 31일
저 자 | Raon Kim
펴낸이 | 한건희
펴낸곳 | 주식회사 부크크
출판사등록 | 2014.07.15(제2014-16호)
주 소 | 서울시 금천구 가산디지털1로 119 SK트윈타워 A동 305호
전 화 | 1670-8316
이메일 | info@bookk.co.kr

ISBN | 979-11-410-2230-3

www.bookk.co.kr
© The Portal Adventrue-Planet L23 2023

The Portal Adventure - Planet L23

By Raon Kim

CONTENTS

Chapter 1

Erica Taylor

Ten years ago, three teenagers named Erica, Bella, and Andrew went on an adventure during their trip to the Grand Canyon. It all started on Erica's birthday.

Erica Taylor was an average teenager with her signature look, long blonde hair, and big blue eyes. She was taller than most kids at her school and enjoyed wearing jeans and comfortable clothes.

She was quite confident and clever and knew the answers to most questions. Everyone would ask, "What do you think, Erica?" Then she could explain the reasons and solutions to them.

Erica lived in an apartment in New York City with her family. She always had a collection of her favorite books in her room. She always dreamed of going on an adventure, like in the books.

At school, she always hung around with Bella Scott and Andrew Lee. Teenager Bella Scott had short, straight dark brown hair and always wore sparkly red-framed glasses. Andrew Lee, ten years ago, was a boy with short, black hair who wore jeans with his favorite lime green T-shirt.

Every lunch break, they would sit on the old brown bench and talk about their new collections of books. All of them simply loved reading books.

"I got myself a new book!" Bella said.

"Cool! What's the title?" Andrew and Erica both looked at her with excitement.

"It's called 'The Adventures of Sarah Smith: The Magic Cave'!" said Bella.

Erica gasped and said, "That's the book I was saving up for!"

"Yeah, but now we could share it together, right?" Bella grinned.

Andrew was so excited that he nearly fell off the bench.

"Be careful!" Bella said.

"You are so clumsy···when will you learn to be careful?" They laughed all the way to the math classroom.

When they arrived, it was twelve-forty, and they still had twenty minutes until the last class of the spring semester, math. Erica sat down on the floor and read her book.

She wished she could take on an adventure someday, like the girl in the book she read. Her life was average, though, until that happened.

Chapter 2

A Birthday Surprise

The bell rang, and break time was over. While having the final exam, Andrew glanced at the big cuckoo clock in Mr. Williams' classroom. He noticed that he only had 10 minutes left to finish the first semester. He whispered to Erica and Bella.

"Psst... It's almost the best time of the year!" he said.

"Great! You know what? I will throw my shoes on the floor tomorrow and sleep until noon." Bella tried hard to stifle a giggle.

But Mr. Williams noticed them talking and laughing.

"Are you serious? You three!" He looked exasperated as he said, "If I see you talking again, I will consider you cheating on the final exam."

Watching the faces of Bella and Andrew, Erica managed to stifle a laugh before it came out and said,

"Yes, Mr. Williams." Erica handed her exam to the teacher.

"Excellent, another full mark, I guess." He winked at her and approached Bella and Andrew.

"Hurry up, you two. Or else you will receive zero marks for the test, and I'm sure your parents won't be so pleased." He walked away, muttering words like 'when will they learn?'

Bella and Andrew worked feverishly to finish the last question. The bell rang again, and the Spring semester was finally over. Mr. Williams said, "All right, everyone! Another semester has passed at lightning speed! I do hope you study math during the summer vacation."

"Well, well... See you guys next semester!" He finished his short speech.

Erica gazed at the calendar. July 20th,

her birthday, is tomorrow. She has been waiting for the day for so long; it felt like ages. Her father promised to take her to the Grand Canyon on her birthday. However, her past few birthdays were bizarre. Either it rained heavily, or hurricanes were approaching. But tomorrow, the weather forecast said it would be warm and sunny.

Most importantly, there's no chance of a hurricane. The good news is that most of the weather forecasts have been accurate recently. This weather may be her chance. And just as she thought, her dad approached her.

He said, "Well, it looks like we are heading to the Grand Canyon tomorrow." Erica was so thrilled she almost threw out the book she was holding.

Erica was speechless for a few minutes and busy organizing her dreamy adventure in her head. After hesitating for a short moment, although it seemed like an hour had passed, she finally asked, "Can...can I bring my friends, Bella and Andrew?"

Her dad smiled and said, "I suppose you can. Anyone else?"

Erica shook her head and said, "Nope, and I bet Mr. Williams won't like it. He doesn't desire long hiking that much." Her dad chuckled.

"Alright! Let's prepare for the adventure, shall we?" Erica smiled at him, walked up the stairs, and reached her room. She couldn't believe what had just happened.

She was going to the Grand Canyon, finally! Everything didn't bother her at all, even the sound of buzzing flies. All was peaceful. Not too long after, Bella and Andrew came to Erica's house with a huge bag of their belongings.

"Gee, what should we pack?" Bella said.

"Don't know. I hope three hiking clothes are enough, though..." Andrew sighed.

"Me too. Let's see. What have we gotten here··· some clothes, toothbrushes, hiking sticks, books, my phone, homework, and some strawberry candies to cheer us up." Bella said, trying to close her bag.

"This thing won't close!" she groaned.

"Yeah, do you call that a few clothing?" Andrew snorted.

"It looks like millions of them!"

Bella glared at him and said, "Well, have you packed your cute stuffed bunny with a big nose?" Bella laughed loudly.

Andrew flushed and retorted. All this bickering, however, didn't bother Erica. Aside from seeing the Grand Canyon, she couldn't wait to see all the other places near the canyon, which looked like miniature toys.

Chapter 3

The Journey to the Grand Canyon

The next day, everyone yawned as they hopped into Taylor's camper. It was one a.m. They put the bags in the car trunk, except for Erica's father, the driver. All the passengers fell asleep as soon as they sat down. It would take about thirty-six hours to get to the Grand Canyon from New York City, and they had a long way to go.

After seven hours, everyone woke up and had breakfast. It was a simple sandwich with ketchup, ham, cheese, lettuce, mustard, and scrambled eggs. Erica's mom always made it when they traveled on the road, her simple recipe worked like magic, and Erica loved them. She always looked forward to road trips because of this sandwich and conversations with everyone.

"What? thirty-six hours!" Andrew exclaimed.

"That's going to take forever!" He looked as though he had got a spider as a birthday present.

"Well, we are planning to stop somewhere in Oklahoma and stay a night. It will take us fourteen hours to get to our destination tomorrow." Erica's dad said.

"There will be a lot of 'Are we there, yet'... scenes." Erica sighed.

"I know you want to get there faster, but we couldn't book a flight ticket. Even if we booked a plane, there's no direct flight to the Grand Canyon. That's a bit of a waste, isn't it?" Erica's mother said.

Fifteen more hours passed. Nearly everyone was asleep. Erica's dad parked the car in the parking lot and woke everyone up to go to the hotel. It was eleven o'clock, so everyone washed and passed out immediately.

After a hasty breakfast in the hotel

restaurant, everyone entered the camper at eight o'clock.

"Fourteen hours to get there..." Andrew yawned. Three hours passed very sluggishly.

"You know what? Within fourteen hours, I could be on the other side of New York on the globe, possibly somewhere in the Indian Ocean. May be Africa or Australia." Andrew said.

"Okay, okay, thank you for your geography lesson, Andrew." Erica and Bella mock Andrew.

"Gosh, I just wanted to say that fourteen hours is a really long time..." Andrew said and sighed.

Chapter 4

The Hole

After eleven more painful hours, the car finally stopped.

"We are here!" said Erica's dad.

Everyone got out of the vehicle. In front of their eyes, the magnificent Grand Canyon was there. Maybe it is massive rock layers, but Erica felt like she was looking at a big castle with stained glass windows and giant diamond chandeliers. Everyone admired it and started talking excitedly.

"Wow, it is way broader than I imagined!" Bella said, staring at the large canyons in the distance.

"It's so cool!" said Andrew, looking impressed.

"I've only seen the canyons in pictures. It's making us feel so small, so we could feel the grandness of nature." Erica exclaimed.

Erica finally managed to come here! Happiness filled her up like having a hot chocolate on some freezing winter day. After gazing at the canyons, everyone unloaded their bags.

"We are able to use the camper now," said Erica's dad.

He opened the door and pressed some buttons. The camper's seats lowered, and now they resembled a thing between a sofa and a small bed. Everyone took their blankets out and put them neatly on the seats.

"So, you did bring your adorable bunny, didn't you?" Bella asked as she stared inside Andrew's bag.

Andrew's bunny is a stuffed animal; he has slept with his bunny since he was seven years old. Andrew flushed and muttered something, but he didn't respond and pulled his blanket up to his head. Erica immediately fell asleep on her seat-bed because the trip had tired her.

The next day, at ten a.m., everyone woke up. "Morning..." said Bella, rubbing her eyes and putting her sparkly red-framed glasses on. Andrew yawned and sank into one of the chairs. Erica, however, was fully awake. She couldn't wait to see the huge canyons!

The morning passed in a hurry. At eleven a.m., everyone wore hiking clothes and had all their hiking gear ready.

"Let's go!" Andrew shouted a bit too loudly. Bella had a look on her face as if she was asking, 'Are you crazy?' Andrew laughed softly as he looked at her.

Everyone ascended the canyons following the travel routes. Three hours had passed, and they had arrived in a big canyon. As Erica had imagined, the rest of the world seemed like a miniature toy at the top of the canyon. The wind tickled her face, and it felt good, and she thought it was peaceful up here.

"Let's go look at the canyons over there," said Andrew, pointing at a canyon with rocks shaped like a star.

"Yeah, I am sure they have a breathtaking view from there." Bella agreed.

Erica hesitated and walked towards the canyon. The view was undoubtedly magnificent, but they were surrounded by star-shaped rocks. Erica thought something was not right; it couldn't be all-natural. Wind couldn't have made identical twenty-six star-shaped rocks, and even carving experts couldn't do it, either.

Bella, who had no clue, said, "Let's take a picture! One, two, three..."

A deafening crash erased the last of Bella's words. The circle with star-shaped rocks around them collapsed and turned into a deep sinkhole. As they fell, Erica caught a glimpse of the object underneath them. It was a swirling mass of blue and purple with sparkling white spots, and it looked like a portal, similar to what she'd seen in movies. As they were close to the ground, Erica closed her eyes, waiting for a crash. She expected her feet to touch a rough surface with intense pain, but it didn't happen. Instead, she landed on something, and it felt like she was standing on a soft cushion...and she reached the bottom of the hole.

Chapter 5

The Place Where Magic Exists

Erica finally opened her eyes. While falling into the hole, she squeezed her eyes shut the whole time. Erica was afraid. She looked around gingerly and saw several significant buildings. But they looked different from the buildings she saw where she lived. The buildings released a robust green glow and were covered with strange plants and devices.

'Where are we? Are we on Earth?' She wondered.

Just as she stood up to investigate, Andrew and Bella were still in a state of unconsciousness.

"Where are we? Are we in heaven?" Andrew woke up and asked.

Bella leaped to her feet and gaped at the strange world they had landed in. Erica looked around and found a dim yellow light that showed a road leading somewhere, looking like a small town. As they decided to walk towards a road, a voice said, "Are you from Earth?" They were startled and turned their heads toward the voice. Then they found a little girl. She had smooth, pink hair and was holding a blue lantern. Erica, Andrew, and Bella nodded. The girl smiled.

"Hello, my name is Lisa. I am the keeper of the portal in the Grand Canyon," she said.

"The thing we passed was a portal? You can't be serious!" Andrew and Bella said.

Lisa smiled and said, "It is perfectly normal not to believe it. You are on planet L23 in the Andromeda galaxy."

Andrew, who still couldn't believe it, said, "Well, how do I know you are not lying?" Lisa's face stiffened.

"I know it is hard to believe, and If you don't trust what I just said, ask around people about where you are!

They will say the same thing!" Lisa said.

Andrew hesitated and said, "Fine." and followed the rest of them to town.

The town was nothing like where they were from, and Erica had fun comparing them. Then, a sudden rumble came from somewhere near them. It had come from Andrew's stomach. Andrew flushed.

"Andrew, your stomach is growling!" Bella giggled.

Lisa smiled and led them to an alley.

It was full of delicious smells, and Lisa gestured for them to enter a small restaurant.

They sat at a small table. The waiter approached them, and Lisa picked up the menu and said, "May I order?" Three nodded in agreement because they knew nothing about the food on L23.

After ten minutes, their food came out. Andrew poked his food and said, "What is this?"

"It's a Sojerf cutlet, like a pork cutlet on Earth, although the texture of the meat is salmon-like," Lisa said.

"It's one of the most delicious foods in here. Lisa added.

"What's this in the pudding?" Erica asked. It looked like a berry, but it was rainbow-colored.

"That's a Suodiou berry. Although it smells like a peach, it tastes like Durian". Lisa said.

After they had finished their meal, they walked out of the restaurant stuffed.

"So, why are we here on this planet?" Bella asked.

"Because you will go to Vera's magic academy, where you can learn how to manage your magical powers," replied Lisa.

There was silence. "But why do we have to be there? We don't have any magical powers, right?" said Erica.

Lisa beamed at them and said, "Then why would you be allowed in this world? Where everyone uses magic."

"Does that mean we could use magic?" Bella said.

"Yeah, like I said, I would be crazy to let someone who doesn't have magical power come into this world," Lisa said.

"Come on, I will take you to the

hotel, and you will stay there," Lisa said and pulled them towards the large building.

Three strangers on L23, Erica, Bella, and Andrew, lay on the bed. They tried to shake off the excitement of attending the magic academy, which kept them from sleeping. Erica's excitement and anticipation for L23 were greater than the night before the Grand Canyon expedition. She couldn't wait to learn everything!

Chapter 6

What Magic Do I Have?

It was their first day at the Magic Academy. Erica, Bella, and Andrew quickly descended the hotel stairs to meet Lisa, who had promised to take them to school. Lisa was waiting in the lobby, smiling radiantly.

"It's always a pleasure to show the way to young students, bringing so many happy memories!" Lisa said.

"Wh···What? Young students?" As Andrew stammered, he wondered, "Why do you sound like an old person?"

"I might look young from your Earth standard, but I will turn two thousand-nine years old this summer. I am the child of a Phoenix family. My mom is a Phoenix, and my dad is an L23 resident." Lisa said authoritatively.

"So... you mean all those kinds of fantasy animals in the books exist here?" Erica said, getting interested.

"Yeah, Unicorns, Phoenixes, the Sphinx... There are many more. People on Earth think those animals are imaginary, but they really exist here." Lisa said.

"Now, come this way. You don't want to be late on the first day." They ran through alleys and main streets until they reached a building where Lisa stopped.

The building was covered with crystals that were shining brightly. There was a large golden dragon-shaped fountain in front of the building. A silver liquid was erupting from it, surrounded by glistening moon-shaped diamond décor. They opened the big door, where they found a giant owl statue. But no doors led them inside the building; all they could see was that giant owl.

"How do we get into the building?"

Erica asked.

"You need a card to enter, but since you are new, I will use my card to let you in today," Lisa replied.

The card was inserted through the beak of the statue of an owl. Suddenly, the owl's beak split into two parts, revealing a large hall in its mouth. Marble covered the hallway, just like outside. As they passed, they saw many classrooms with jade doors. After passing countless jade doors, they reached the top level, which was the principal's office.

"Lavina, I have brought some newly enrolled students," Lisa said.

The door opened. A young lady stood before them. The lady had dark purple hair and wore a black mini-dress with a stiff collar. She smiled and brought them into the classroom. 'She doesn't look like the typical principal we see on Earth.' Erica thought.

"You could sit here." She pointed at

the three lavish marble tables with chairs near the window.

"You will receive an education in the foundation of magic here. Each of you will need a card to enter," she said, giving them the cards made of silver with the big letter 'V' in the middle.

As they looked around the classroom, they encountered many students. A student with horns and sparkly black hair roasted marshmallows by breathing fire. Another student with dazzling wings and a rainbow horn flew around the room. A girl with nine tails and long flowing black hair turned into a nine-tail fox and curled up on her chair. A boy, who had the body of a horse, was playing the harp, and this made them more excited.

The bell rang. Lavina left, and a teacher came. She had two pairs of glittery wings and held a fairy wand with flowers blooming repeatedly. When she entered the classroom, the class became silent at once.

"Good morning." the teacher said, smiling.

"I hope you are ready for our class," she said.

"But first, since we have newcomers. Let's introduce ourselves. My name is Gloria, and I'm a fairy. I look after the forests." she said, showing off her wings to the class.

A girl raised her hands and said, "My name is Evelyn. I am half-unicorn, and I love flying."

A boy who had been playing the harp before class said, "My name is Alexander. I am a Centaurus, and my hobby is playing the harp."

After everyone else had introduced themselves, it was Erica's turn.

"Um···I am from a planet called Earth with Bella and Andrew. I like reading books." she said.

Erica's story might sound typical on Earth, but everyone else in the class seemed interested. After an hour, recess started. Many students gathered around Erica, Bella, and Andrew.

"What do you eat there?" one student asked. Other students asked questions such as, "what do you do for fun?" and "what games do you play?"

They spent the whole recess answering questions from the students.

Later that day, the three learned how to make balls of power and aim them at the target. When making the power balls, they didn't notice which power they had except Bella, whose power was fire.

Erica accidentally shot a lizard with her power during her practice in the hotel. When she leaned closer to the lizard, the lizard said, "Watch where you shoot, young lady!" Erica stared at it. Suddenly, the lizard could talk! Maybe she had the power to make animals talk.

"I'm sorry. Will you come with me to dinner?" Erica asked.

"Of course! Wonder what the menu

is." the lizard said, hopping onto Erica's shoulder.

While they had dinner, Andrew talked about how he found the power he had.

"While I was just looking at the sky, I fell down because I was leaning on the window too closely. I wanted help from someone but couldn't scream because I was too scared. Then, a vine caught me and wrapped it around my body to support me. Then I realized that I have the power to control plants!" And indeed, he made a pot plant nearby to do a twist dance. Erica sat down and let Mr. Lizard go from her shoulder.

"Hi, friends. What's for dinner?" Bella and Andrew froze, and Erica had to explain to them the power she had.

"It's so cool! Can you make my cat talk when we get back?" Bella asked.

"Speaking of home, I miss my parents," Andrew said, sighing.

"Me too. It is fun here, but I miss my regular routines back home." Erica said.

"There is no better place than home," Bella said, nodding.

"So, then, what are we waiting for? Let's find the way home!"

Mr. Lizard said, heading towards their luggage.

"Hold on for a second. How do we get back home?" Erica asked, pulling Mr. Lizard away.

"Let's ask Lisa. She will know what to do." Andrew answered.

They packed their belongings and headed towards Lisa's home, which she had told them earlier. It was a small wooden house near the academy.

Chapter 7

Lisa's Plan

They knocked on the door where Lisa lived. After a few seconds, Lisa came out.

"Oh, it's you guys. What brings you here?" she asked, opening the door.

"Come in!" she said, smiling.

They stepped inside the house. The house was tiny yet cozy. The shelves were full of flower-patterned kitchen utensils and pastries shaped like hearts. Lisa offered them some of her pastries and brought out a bright mint-colored tea, which tasted just like hot chocolate.

"So, why did you decide to come here? You couldn't have come for no reason, right?" Lisa said.

"Yeah⋯Lisa, we are having so much

fun here, but now we want to return home." Erica said.

Soon as Erica finished her sentence, Lisa's warm smile on her face disappeared quickly. It made the three of them get goosebumps as she suddenly changed her look.

Lisa screamed, "You won't be returning home!" and pushed the button near her. Then black ropes came down and tied them around tightly.

"You will never return home if I put you in the attic and lock the door!" Lisa said.

None of them had expected this, and they had thought Lisa was an excellent helper. Now before them stood a girl with an evil smile.

Now Erica, Bella, and Andrew were helpless in the dusty grey attic. Soon after hearing someone unlock the padlock, Lisa entered the room.

"Do you remember when I said that

I am the daughter of the Phoenix family? Our family was banned from this planet and lived on Earth long ago. However, I was able to get back." Lisa said.

When Lisa was a child, a jealous man Lisa's family believed was a true friend put her family into so much trouble. He framed Lisa's father as a traitor, and as a result, the whole family was forced to leave planet L23. Lisa's family legacy and the reputation they built for millions of years evaporated completely. No other planets welcomed her family, so they settled on Earth.

"The people on Earth treated us brutally. Now, it's your turn to taste the pain I had. I knew you would miss home one day and be homesick, and I have been waiting for the moment you will beg to return home, so I can make you suffer more." Lisa's voice became icy and flat as she continued.

"What will your parents say? They have probably spent sleepless nights since you left." Lisa asked, her eyes glistening with madness and excitement.

"Lisa, I understand what your family has suffered and truly feel sorry. But this is mad! Why do you hold resentment against us?" asked Andrew.

"No! Do you think I tried to punish you three? Only three of you?" Lisa laughed sarcastically and said,

"I will ensure that every living thing on Earth is extinguished by not letting you finish your mission."

"Mission? Are we here on a mission? What are you talking about?" Erica asked, her voice has terribly trembled from fear.

"Soon, you'll need to find the three sacred objects scattered around the seven continents of L23. If you fail the mission, your planet will vanish helplessly." Lisa replied.

"So, all we need to do is find those

three sacred things, correct?" Andrew asked.

"Of course, haha. Guess you think this will be a simple task, huh? Go find the sacred objects, you clueless humans! I bet you could never leave this place." Lisa sneered. She left the room, laughing hysterically.

"What do we do now? Did Lisa mention seven continents? I mean, how big is this L23 planet?" Bella whispered.

I wish we had learned how to combine our powers earlier because now that we're trapped here, we can't learn how to do it!" Andrew said.

"What should we do now?" Erica said.

While they were thinking and discussing the solution, Mr. Lizard got through the door and brought scissors. As soon as he put them in his mouth, he began cutting the ropes. In the distance, they could hear Lisa stepping into her room. Inside the attic, everyone moved fast. First, they tried to turn the doorknob, and as they guessed, the door was locked.

"I got an idea!" Erica said, pulling her hairpin out.

It took quite a while, but the door finally opened, and they exited the attic. As everyone walked towards the main entrance, Andrew spotted a familiar object. The portal maker! Lisa last showed it to them when they were invited to dinner at Lisa's.

"Look what I found!" Andrew called

everyone to show them the portal maker.

Compared to its majestic function, the portal maker is relatively small and light in weight. It was designed to be portable so that anyone could hold it with one hand.

"That's great! We will get to where we want to go with the portal maker! There may be more clues here that we can find. Possibly the location of sacred things." Erica suggested.

"Wait, if I had to hide something im -portant, I would keep it in my room. I have a feeling that Lisa keeps clues in her room." Bella shared her idea.

While looking around the room for clues about the three sacred items' location, they spotted the map in the room where Lisa was sleeping. Even though Lisa was sleeping soundly, everyone tipped their toes and tried not to make any noise. In absolute silence, the bedroom floor squeaked. They were about to be found. As they exited Lisa's room, they hid in the bathroom.

"What do we do now? Lisa will be woken up by a squeaky floor again! Wish we were smaller⋯." Andrew said.

"Hmm, that's it! We could get help from the little guy, Mr. Lizard!" Erica said.

So, Mr. Lizard climbed into the room and slipped through the door. He used his feet as suction cups and brought the map outside safely. Now, they can use the map and travel around the planet to stop the Earth from collapsing.

Erica wrapped the portal maker carefully with the map they found to protect. As she put the portal maker in her pocket, Erica felt movement.

"Bella, Andrew! Did you feel it too?" Erica asked in a confused voice.

"Felt what?" Andrew answered.

Erica put her hand in her pocket to see if the portal was still safe. When she put out the portal maker, it activated automatically. And again, Erica, Bella, and Andrew slid down to the portal.

Chapter 8

The Three Sacred Things

"Hang in there! We are about to land." Andrew shouted.

When the portal disappeared, they were on a busy street in Acuario. According to the map, L23 has seven continets, and Acuario is the largest among them.

Erica asked with a concerned look, "Are you guys okay? No one was injured, right?".

"I can't see Mr. Lizard! He is gone!" Bella replied.

"He must have jumped from my shoulder when we fell into the portal. It is better for him, and I am sure he will be safe." Erica sighed.

"It's a blessing that we escaped from Lisa's house, but how can we find the sacred thing? "We need to cover a lot of areas," Andrew said.

"I think there is a reason why we are here on this continent. We will have to search for clues first." Bella said.

Erica answered, "Clues can be something symbolic. Like souvenirs, they are good representations of a country or town."

They looked around the local stores in the market nearby. Among the souvenirs was a miniature statue of a boy pouring water from an antique jug. It was an Aquarius sign!

"This might be the one!" Erica said.

"Look, Erica, in your pocket!" Bella tapped Erica's shoulder and pointed at Erica's pocket.

The portal maker glowed, and an old marble water bottle image appeared before them when they approached the Aquarius statue. As they touched it, the image transformed into Libra.

"Next clue is Libra. No wonder there are many pairs of scales in the old market." Andrew sounded delighted.

They soon learned that the pair of scales was the sacred thing here. The portal maker, however, did not respond. When the portal maker whizzed, a beam of light came out, and it pointed at a piece of gold and blood-red garnet that looked like a set of scales.

"Do we have to take the whole statue?" Andrew asked.

"Impossible! It is almost the size of a human being. I don't think three of us can lift it." Bella said.

Erica looked around, sure that the Libra statue was not the only thing noticeable there. Like a button, she found a tiny blue mark carved into the ground. There was only one mark on that statue, and Erica pushed the impression as hard as she could. Suddenly, a small pair of scales appeared exactly like the statue but much smaller. Erica caught it with her hands and held it tightly.

Then, the portal maker glowed again; this time, the portal took them to Geminis. The continent is in the Far East of the planet on L23. Once they landed, they were in the middle of a rice field. The continent of Geminis is a farming land with no souvenir stores.

"What should we do?" Bella asked.

"No hints," Andrew said, shaking his head.

Suddenly, the portal maker created another portal leading to the narrow one. They walked in, and it was a cave. They walked into the cave until the cave started emitting red light. There was a book at the end of the light path. They tried to figure out what was the source of the red light from the portal. While they explored the surroundings,

Bella held the book and started to read. It was a typical folktale about two sisters. Ultimately, the two sisters who worked together in hard times became wealthy and happy.

"This book was interesting, but what connection does it have to our mission?" Andrew said.

"Don't know. Well, the book cover said it was the seventh edition, and maybe there's a connection between this book and the number seven." Erica replied.

Bella closed and opened the book seven times to see what would happen.

"Nothing. Just old paper," Bella said.

As they were about to turn away, the book's words scattered in the air, clearing the page completely. On the empty page, the number seven appeared shortly after. It was then that a necklace of two sisters appeared on a pendant. Erica jumped and caught the pendant before it fell to the ground.

"That pendant is the third sacred thing, right?" Andrew asked.

They thought they had found all the sacred things on the three continents. But nothing happened. Suddenly, the portal maker showed them the universe with many stars and planets. In the blink of an eye, everything disappeared from their view, and they have transported again.

Chapter 9

Estrella

When they landed, their surroundings turned dark blue.

"Why are we here? Don't tell me there is another thing to find," Bella said.

"Well, leaving that problem aside,where are we?" Andrew asked.

"Looks like we are in···the ocean? What?" Erica gasped.

They were standing inside a transparent device shaped like a bubble. Perhaps it is some sort of submarine that looks like a giant bubble. As they look out of the bubble, they are in the mythical blue ocean. There are no currents or sea creatures, and the water feels serene. As the device navigated itself, it sank gradually until it stopped in front of an underwater cave. At the cave entrance is a sign that says 'Estrella.'

Before they could do anything, the bubble moved deeper and deeper into the cave. When they finally stopped, the three sacred objects collected from the three continents floated in the middle and slipped into the sockets. The cave rumbled and made a portal on the ground. As they wondered what was happening around them, golden writing appeared on the floor. 'The Earth has stopped collapsing. You may

go home.'

"You see what I see, right?" Andrew rubbed his eyes to see if he was dreaming.

"We could finally go home!" Bella shouted.

"What are you waiting for? Let's go!" Erica shouted.

The moment they were about to jump into the portal, someone in a long dark cloak appeared, also in a bubble, blocking their way.

"I have got you!" the person said. The person took off the cloak. It was Lisa.

Chapter 10

Back to Earth

"Lisa?" Erica said blankly.

"Yes, you remember me?" Lisa answered.

"I noticed you had escaped. I guess you thought you would be free after leaving my house, huh? I am not that naive." Lisa smiled.

"I put a tracking device on the portal maker you had always held."

"Now, it's time for us to say goodbye. Any last words?" Lisa said.

She made a tornado out of her fingertips. She whirled her index finger around the bubble device. The bubble got thinner and thinner and created cracks everywhere. Water started to come in and filled two-thirds of the bubble.

"What do we do now? We are going to drown!" Bella exclaimed.

The cave started transforming into a gigantic ball-shaped submarine just as the water poured in. Lisa was left behind since the submarine only took three friends. Lisa's bubble turned into a prison and locked her up. Lisa yelled at them, but they couldn't hear a thing. Within a minute, a portal appeared on the submarine's ceiling. Erica, Bella, and Andrew once again drifted into a portal. The inside of the portal is surrounded by star-shaped rocks, just like the one they entered. Once they got in, everything turned dark.

When they landed, they were in the same canyon they had been in. Erica's mom and dad were standing in the same spot and gazing at the canyons, just like when they fell into the first portal. Erica checked the time, and it was 2:41.

"Mom? Dad? Did you see that thing?"

Erica asked.

"What thing? Are you talking about the eagle flying over the peak?" Erica's dad replied.

Erica, Bella, and Andrew looked at each other puzzled.

"Mr. Taylor, how long have we gone?" Andrew asked.

"Gone? Gone where? I saw the three of you standing there the whole time." Erica's dad answered.

This time Bella asked Erica's mom, "Mrs. Taylor, so we got here like a minute ago, right?"

"Yes! Wait···what are your plans, you three? Stop right here if you are trying to pull some pranks on us. Let us enjoy this moment, and you should too." Erica's mom replied.

Would it be possible for the three of us to have a daydream at the same time? I am sure the questions and the looks on their faces meant Bella and Andrew had experienced what I had experienced.' Erica was busy figuring out what had just happened.

After a long silence, Andrew broke the silence. "That was a phenomenal adventure!"

"Yeah, but I wish it was real.." Erica sighed.

Erica felt something in her pocket as they tried to hike back to where they had started. She put her hand in to see what was inside, and she could feel an object. And it was very familiar. It was the portal maker! Erica carefully held the portal maker as she took it out. She approached Bella and Andrew and showed them what she was holding. They briefly glanced and noticed what it was right away. And the three were quiet all the way until they reached their base camp.

Epilogue

A New Adventure

The Grand Canyon was crowded with people. Three people in their twenties silently took out what they had used ten years ago. They got up to the canyon with the pointy twenty-six star-shaped rocks, looked around to see if anyone was watching them, and clicked the button. A bluish, greenish light appeared in the middle of nowhere as they activated the thing. It was the portal. The three people walked toward the light without saying a word.

Everything around them turned pitch black. When the darkness cleared, Lavina stood there, waiting for the visitors. "Welcome back to planet L23, Erica, Bella, and Andrew!"

The Author's Story

Hi, this is Raon Kim from South Korea. I am an elementary school student in Suwon, and I started writing my first book in 2021.

If you ask me what my favorite genre is, it's fantasy books, and that's why I started writing a fantasy book that you will read.

Have you ever considered that unicorns, dragons, and other fantasy animals are real? Your parents told you there were no fantasy animals?

In this book, there is a planet called L23 where all kinds of fantasy animals exist. The main characters, Erica, Bella, and Andrew, find a portal while traveling. They have fun, but something turns out wrong.

I am thankful for the people who helped me write this book. So, I hope you enjoy reading this book and thinking about what will happen next! Thank you!